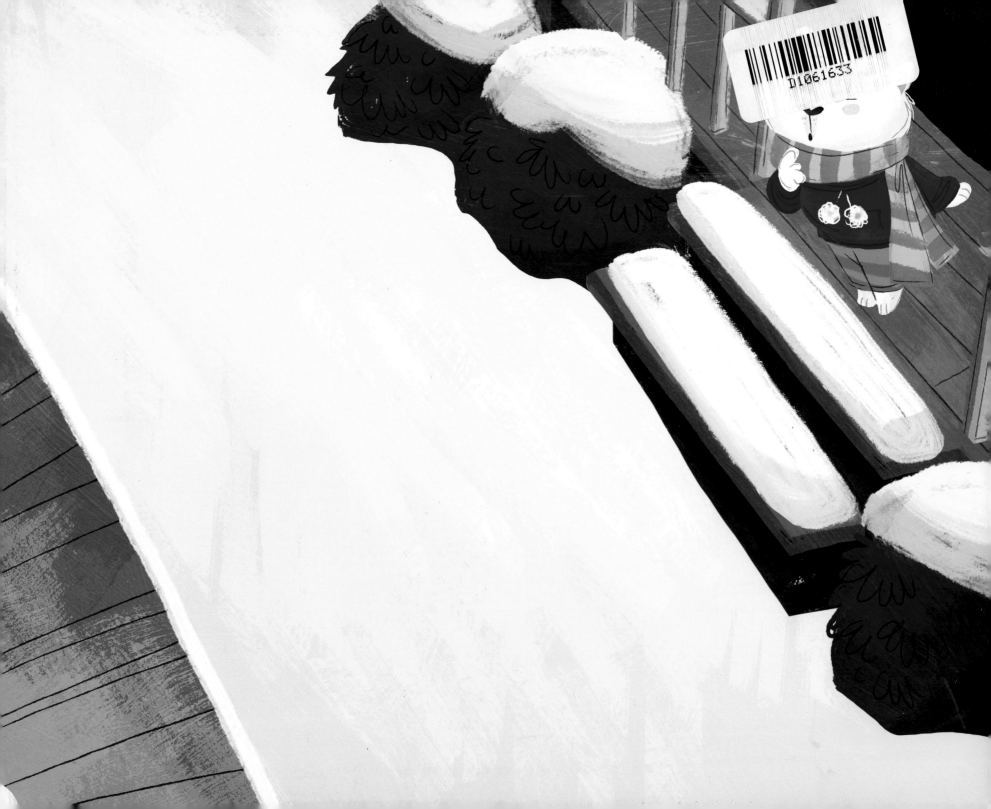

For my just so perfect boys—
Joe, Ben, and Jason.— SS

For Dash & Otter, my just so perfect
little muses. Rise & fly, sweet spirits.— SL

STERLING CHILDREN'S BOOKS
New York

An Imprint of Sterling Publishing Co., Inc.
1166 Avenue of the Americas
New York, NY 10036

STERLING CHILDREN'S BOOKS and the distinctive Sterling Children's Books logo
are registered trademarks of Sterling Publishing Co., Inc.

Text © 2019 Sara F. Shacter
Illustrations © 2019 Stephanie Laberis

All rights reserved. No part of this publication may be reproduced, stored in a retrieval system,
or transmitted in any form or by any means (including electronic, mechanical, photocopying,
recording, or otherwise) without prior written permission from the publisher.

ISBN 978-1-4549-2741-9

Distributed in Canada by Sterling Publishing Co., Inc.
c/o Canadian Manda Group, 664 Annette Street
Toronto, Ontario M6S 2C8, Canada
Distributed in the United Kingdom by GMC Distribution Services
Castle Place, 166 High Street, Lewes, East Sussex BN7 1XU, England
Distributed in Australia by NewSouth Books
University of New South Wales, Sydney, NSW 2052, Australia

For information about custom editions, special sales, and premium and corporate purchases, please contact
Sterling Special Sales at 800-805-5489 or specialsales@sterlingpublishing.com.

Manufactured in China

Lot #:
2 4 6 8 10 9 7 5 3 1
07/19

sterlingpublishing.com

Cover and interior design by Jo Obarowski

Just So
WILLOW

by SARA F. SHACTER

illustrated by STEPHANIE LABERIS

STERLING CHILDREN'S BOOKS
New York

Willow liked things just so.

She ironed her underwear.

She unscrambled her spaghetti.

She tidied her teacher.

One morning, while Willow dusted her
bubblegum collection, snow began to fall.
Her backyard sat safely tucked under a crisp,
white sheet. It was just so perfect.

Laughs and shouts tumbled over the fence.

Willow watched kids from her block running and rolling, stomping and sliding—making a lumpy, bumpy mess! It was just so awful.

"I'll stay inside," she told herself, "so my snow stays smooth and clean."

A snowball sailed through the air . . . closer and closer, until . . .

SPLAT!

"Hey! You're messing up my yard!"

But with all the running and rolling and stomping and sliding, nobody heard. Willow stamped her paw. "They're not turning my yard into a lumpy, bumpy mess!"

Willow barreled down the stairs, onto the porch—
and stopped.

The snow! She'd ruin it!

Willow stayed put. "Stop throwing those snowballs!" she yelled.

No one yelled back.

"How can I get closer so they'll hear me?" Willow spotted her swing set.

"I could jump!"

But if she missed . . .

Willow charged across the porch,

launched—

and dangled.

Then she pulled and pumped.
She bellowed and blustered.
She hooted and hollered.

Nobody hollered back.
"I have to get closer!"

Willow eyed the tree. A thick branch stretched over the fence—the perfect perch!

But if she fell . . .

She cut and tied . . .

lassoed the branch . . .

lassoed another . . .

and kicked off the trunk . . .

Willow grinned. "Woooo hoooooo!!!!!"
She looked back. A crisp, white ribbon wrapped
around the yard. It was just so perfect.

With her new friends,
Willow vroomed and zoomed,

packed and stacked,

rollicked and frolicked.

When the sun sank low in the sky,
Willow's friends sent her gliding home.

A crisp, white line cut across her yard.

A just-so-perfect path to follow the next day.